Tears of a Friend

I am furious.

'What is my style? Looking boring? Being covered up? Wearing the cheap versions of your clothes? Oh, I know what my style is. It's to make you look better when you stand next to me. Thanks a lot!' I say. Claire's mouth hangs open.

Tears of a Friend

Look out for other exciting stories
in the *Sharp Shades* series:

A Murder of Crows by Penny Bates
Shouting at the Stars by David Belbin
Witness by Anne Cassidy
Doing the Double by Alan Durant
Blitz by David Orme
Plague by David Orme
Hunter's Moon by John Townsend

Tears of a Friend

By Joanna Kenrick
Adapted by David Belbin

Published by Evans Brothers Limited
2A Portman Mansions
Chiltern St
London W1U 6NR

British Library Cataloguing in Publication Data
Kenrick, Joanna
    Tears of a friend. - Differentiated ed. - (Sharp
    shades)
    1. Friendship - Fiction 2. Young adult fiction
    I. Title
    823.9'2[J]

ISBN-13: 9780237535254

Series Editor: David Belbin
Editor: Julia Moffatt
Designer: Rob Walster
Picture research: Bryony Jones

This abridged edition was first published in its
original form as a *Shades* title of the same name.

Picture acknowledgements:
istockphoto.com: 8, 12, 18, 25, 29, 34, 35, 44, 49
and 61

Contents

Chapter One

'It's not fair,' says my best friend Claire. 'Midnight isn't late.'

Claire is fourteen, like me. Unlike me, she's really pretty. She has long blonde hair. Boys love it.

She looks like a model.

'You're not listening, Cassie! They grounded me for a week!'

'Didn't they say you had to be in by eleven?' I ask.

'Whose side are you on?' Claire snaps. 'I had to go to Nick's gig.'

Nick is her older brother. I fancy him rotten but would never say.

'Was it good?' I ask.

'Brilliant. I met this hot bloke.'

I knew it. The school bell rings. We pick up our bags.

'Did you know Louise is having a party?' says Claire.

'Really? When?'

'Next Thursday. It's for her sister.'

'Why?'

'She passed her driving test at last.'

We grin at each other. We don't like Louise's sister. We found it very funny when she failed three times.

'Will your parents let you go?' I ask.

'Who cares? I'm going anyway.'

'I was thinking about Louise's party,' Claire says after Maths. She sighs. I know what's coming. 'I've got nothing to wear.'

We always go through this. Claire's wardrobe is twice the size of mine. She has loads of nice shoes

too. Loads more then me.

I have grown out of my one decent dress. Not upwards, just outwards.

'I've got nothing to wear either,' I say.

Claire cheers up. 'Let's go shopping!'

Chapter Two

There's a new shopping centre near me. It's got Top Shop and Miss Selfridge. There are some funky little boutiques too. I always spend too much.

'Over here, Cassie!' calls Claire. She looks stunning as usual. Pink crop-top and tight jeans.

'Oh my God!' I gasp. 'Have you had your belly-button pierced?'

'Fooled you!' Claire shows me the little jewel. 'It's stick-on. I bought it just now.'

'It looks really cool,' I say. Now I want one too. But that would be copying. And my tummy isn't flat like hers.

'Come on, there's some new stuff in Top Shop.'

We have a brilliant time. I love trying on clothes. We go to Dorothy

Perkins. Claire puts on this dress that looks amazing. I pull on a dark green velvet top. I gasp at myself in the mirror. I look fantastic. The top is very low cut. I have a cleavage.

I turn to Claire. 'What do you think?'

'Hang on a minute,' she says. 'Does this make me look fat?'

'No,' I say, 'but look at me!'

'It's all right.' She's looking at herself again.

I'm angry. 'Look properly!' I say loudly.

Claire looks surprised. And a bit annoyed. But she does look at me.

'It's nice. Bit revealing though, isn't it? For you, I mean.'

'What do you mean, for me?'

I feel hot, red anger boil up inside me.

'It's just not your style.'

I am furious.

'What is my style? Looking boring? Being covered up? Wearing the cheap versions of your clothes? Oh, I know what my style is. It's to make you look better when you stand next to me. Thanks a lot!' I say. Claire's mouth hangs open.

I storm out of the changing room. I fling the top at the shop assistant.

'No thanks,' I say. 'It's not my style.'

What an exit!

I am very impressed with myself. For about five minutes. When I get home I burst into tears. I'm angry with myself and with Claire. Maybe I can make it up with Claire tomorrow? But why should I?

Chapter Three

I haven't seen Claire since Saturday.
On Monday, Mr Price tries to make
us work together.

'I'd rather not work with Cassie,'
says Claire. She won't look at me.

'All right,' says Mr Price, surprised. I pretend not to mind.

At break I have no one to talk to. I've never needed any other friends. Now I wish I'd made the effort.

Over the next few days I make friends with Isabel, the nerdy girl in the class. She's so grateful, it makes me feel sorry for her. She has even less confidence than me. That annoys me. I wish she'd stand up for herself a bit. Is this how Claire thinks of me?

Even Mum sees something odd.

'Where's Claire these days?' she says. 'I haven't seen her for ages.'

'We're not friends any more,' I say.

She doesn't ask again.

The day before the party, I decide something. It's time to make some changes. Maybe Claire's right. I should make more of an effort with the way I look. Then I'd be more popular.

I go back to Dorothy Perkins and buy the green velvet top.

Chapter Four

I nearly decide not to go to the
party. But why should Claire stop
me having a good time?

I pull on the dark green velvet
top. It does make me look amazing. I

decide to wear a short black skirt. I
spend ages on my make-up. I'm not
very good at it yet. I put too much
eye-shadow on and look like I've got
two black eyes.

There's not much I can do with my
hair. It always ends up a frizzy mess. I
put loads of mousse on. It looks nice
but feels bad, like dry glue.

'You look nice,' says my mum.

'Thanks.' I wonder if she means
it. She doesn't like me wearing
short skirts.

'Who has a party on a school
night?' she asks. 'None of you will be
fit for school in the morning. Be no

later than eleven. And get someone
to walk you home, or call me.'

'Yes, Mum.'

At Louise's door, I hear a shout.

'Hey, Cassie!' It's Isabel. I didn't
think she was coming. But here she
is, wearing four-inch heels. She has
a fishnet top over a black vest. And
she's even worse at make-up than I
am. I have to go into the party with
her. People will think we came
together. I ring the door bell.

Chapter Five

It's not Louise who opens the door.
It's some boy I don't know.

'Hi,' he says. His eyes are kind of
red. 'Come in.'

Isabel and I step into the hall.

There's a crowd of people.

'Come on!' calls Isabel. 'The fun's always in the kitchen!' She pushes her way in. I stay where I am. There are a lot of people I don't know. Most of them are older than me.

Then my heart stops. It's Nick, Claire's brother. He's wearing a leather jacket and holding a cigarette. He looks amazing.

'Hi,' I say. 'I'm Cassie, Claire's friend.'

Nick turns to look at me, and I do something stupid. I put my hand out. To shake hands with him.

'Oh yeah, hi,' he says. He ignores

my hand.

'How are you? I hear your gig went well last week.'

Nick stares at me.

'Yeah, it was cool.' He takes a swig from a beer. His eyes slide down. 'Nice top,' he says. Then he goes into the front room.

I try to pull my top up higher. I should feel pleased he liked it, but I feel dirty. I didn't like the way he looked at me. I head to the kitchen.

I push past a couple snogging by the stairs.

'Sorry,' I say.

'Watch where you're going,' snaps

the girl. It's Claire. Her eyes open wide when she sees me. Then she starts kissing the boy again. It's not someone I know. I go past them, feeling sick.

The kitchen is buzzing. There's a funny smell in the air, like Mum's musk perfume. I pour myself a coke and try not to catch anyone's eye. Why did I come?

'Hi, sexy,' says a boy with dark hair. He looks about eighteen, and his eyes are on my cleavage. 'Want to have a bit of fun?' He shows me a plastic bag. It looks like it's full of dried leaves. Weed.

'No thank you.'

'Go on. You look like the kind of girl who needs to relax.'

He's very tall, and leaning over me.

'No,' I say, but my mouth has gone dry. He looks at my cleavage again and reaches out a hand. I freeze. I want to move but I can't.

'Hiya, Cassie,' says a cheerful voice from behind him. 'Fancy some fresh air?' A hand takes my wrist.

Chapter Six

When we're out of the kitchen I can breathe. I look at my rescuer.

'Mark!' He's in my class at school but I don't know him that well.

'You looked a bit desperate,' he

says, letting go of my wrist. 'Hope I did the right thing.'

'Yeah, thanks,' I say.

'You don't have to go outside with me. I just wanted to get you away from that bloke.'

'No, I'd like to,' I yell. 'It's too hot in here.'

As we head out the front door, we

pass a couple going upstairs.

'Isn't that your friend Claire?'
Mark says.

Claire is giggling. The guy she was
snogging has his hand on her bum.
Her skirt is up around her waist.

'Somebody got lucky,' grins Mark.

I follow Mark into the front
garden. I take big gulps of air.

'Are you all right?' Mark asks. I sit down.

'I'm fine. Honest.'

Mark sits down next to me. I don't know what to say. I'm worried about Claire, going to a bedroom with a stranger. I wonder about Mark. Why did he rescue me? Will he want something in return? He's nice, I guess, but I don't really fancy him. Does he fancy me? My head hurts.

'I hate parties,' Mark says suddenly.

'What?'

'Parties. Silly clothes. Everyone drinks too much to show they're cool. They get off with people they don't even like. It stinks.'

'I know what you mean!' I say.
'What's so cool about throwing up
all night?'

We grin at each other.

'Why did we come?' Mark asks.

'I don't know.'

'I like being out here, though,' he
says.

'Me too. We can watch everyone
else making fools of themselves.'

'Excellent.' He produces a bottle
of lemonade from behind his back.
'Want another really uncool drink?'

'Definitely.'

Chapter Seven

Mark and I chat easily. I don't have any friends that are boys but Mark's okay. I can tell he's not going to grope me, or try to snog me. We talk about school, friends, family. I even tell him about my row with Claire.

Half an hour later a girl runs out of the front door. She's got no shoes on. It's Claire. She nearly trips. I find myself going to help her.

'Claire, are you okay?'

She stares at me like she's never seen me before.

'Get off me, get off me!' she screams.

She stumbles into the road. I follow her.

'Claire, are you okay?' I can't think of anything else to say. She's not okay. She looks awful. 'What's happened?'

Claire ignores me and hurries off down the road. I turn to Mark.

'What should we do?'

'Nothing,' he says. 'You can't help someone who doesn't want to be helped. Does she live nearby?'

'Yeah, the next street.'

'Then she'll be home in a minute. She'll be all right.'

I'm not so sure.

Chapter Eight

It's only ten. Mum's surprised I'm home so early. She likes the look of Mark, I can tell.

'Thanks so much for walking her home,' she says.

Mark gives me a wink as he goes.
'See you tomorrow, Cassie.'

'Yeah.' I give a bit of a grin. Then
I make an excuse about being tired
and head to my room. It takes me
ages to get to sleep. I keep thinking
about Claire.

She's not at school for registration.
Or break. Or lunch. I can't think
clearly. Mark tries to talk to me in
French but I'm too busy thinking
about Claire. He gets told off.

After school I go straight round to
Claire's house. Claire's dad opens
the door. He works from home.

'We haven't seen you for a while. Have you come to see Claire?' He frowns. 'I hope you can be a good influence on her. We caught her coming back from a party last night. She was supposed to be grounded.'

'Oh,' I say blankly.

'I don't know what we're going to do. She doesn't listen to us any more. Go on up. She's just got home from school.'

I don't say anything. He can't know Claire wasn't in school today.

Claire's door has a 'Do Not Disturb' sign on the handle. What if she doesn't want to see me? I knock and go in.

'Claire? It's me.'

Claire is on her bed, knees up to her chin. She's got her back to the door.

'I knew it was you,' she says. 'I'm surprised Dad let you in. He's in a right mood with me.'

She doesn't turn round. I sit on the side of the bed.

'Are you okay?' I ask. 'Only, you weren't in school today.'

She sits up at this.

'Keep your voice down. I would have stayed home but Dad would have been on at me. I pretended to go out as usual.'

'Where did you go?'

'What do you care? I thought you were fed up with being my shadow?'

'That doesn't mean I don't care about you. I was worried.' I feel really cross with her. I stand up. 'But if you'd rather I went, have it your way.' I turn to go.

'No, Cassie, wait!' I stop.

'Don't go, Cass. I need to talk to someone. Please. I have to tell someone.'

I walk back to the bed. 'Go on then. What happened at the party?'

She takes a deep breath.

'That boy – he tried to make me have sex with him.'

Chapter Nine

My face must show how worried I am.
Quickly, she says, 'I'm all right.
Honest. I was a bit shaken up,
that's all.'

'You'd better start from the

beginning.'

'You saw me with that guy by the stairs,' Claire says. I nod. 'He seemed really nice. He goes to school with Louise's sister. He seemed to like me. I didn't have anyone to talk to. Normally, I'd talk to you.'

She looks sad. I know what she means. But I don't want to talk about our row. It seems silly now.

'It doesn't matter,' I say. 'Go on.'

'I was flattered. He could have had anyone. He said his name was Pete. I told him I was sixteen.'

'Claire!'

'He wouldn't be interested if he

knew I was fourteen. He kept getting me drinks. I think he put something in the coke. I started to find everything really funny. And then he said, "Do you want a tour of the house?" '

I groan.

'I know, I know,' Claire sighs. 'Anyway, he took me straight into a bedroom. Then I sort of tripped over, and we both fell on the bed. I was laughing so much I wasn't worried. Then he put his hand up my skirt.'

'What did you do?'

Claire looks at me, her eyes big and swimmy.

'I didn't know what to do. I tried

to move his hands away. Then I
thought, maybe I should let him.
After all, I did snog him. And I did
like him, sort of. Maybe I led him
on. I should have said no right at
the beginning, not halfway through.'

I shake my head.

'You can say no at any point.
That's what my mum always says.'

'When he saw I wasn't going to
let him, he said I owed him. He said
he couldn't stop. He said once boys
got started they couldn't stop.'

'That's not true, is it?' I say.

'I don't know. I kept pushing him
away. He was so much stronger,

Cassie. I couldn't do anything. I got
tired of fighting him off. Then
Louise came in.'

Chapter Ten

'Louise?'

'She went mad. Turns out we were in her parents' room. She was yelling, "Didn't we have any respect?"'

I let out a giggle. I can't help it.

'What did Pete say?'

'I don't know,' Claire says. 'He was looking for his trousers. I grabbed my bag and ran out.' Claire grins. 'Last I saw, Louise was hitting him on the head with her mum's box of tissues.'

We laugh and laugh and roll on the bed. We're laughing instead of crying. Claire's dad pops his head in to see what all the noise is about.

'Glad to see you two have made up.'

We laugh even more at this. How could such a horrible thing bring us back together?

In the end, we calm down. We lie on the bed together.

'Are you going to tell anyone?' I ask.

'Like who?'

'The police or something.' Shouldn't you tell your parents?'

'Are you mad? After the fuss they made last night?'

'He might do it again. To someone else.'

Claire thinks for a minute. 'No. It must have been me. I got myself into that mess. I should have been firmer at the start.'

Was it her fault? She was wearing

a really short skirt. Inside my head, I hear Mum say, 'Whenever you say no, it means no. Whatever you've said yes to before. No means no.'

'You told him to stop,' I said. 'You were fighting him off. He knew what he was doing was wrong. It's not your fault.'

'We were both drunk. He didn't manage to do anything anyway. I made a mistake. I'll know next time.'

We both stare at the ceiling for a while.

'What about you?' Claire asks. 'Did you have a good time?'

I grin. 'I met this boy…'

'Cassie!'

'Nothing happened. Actually, it was Mark from our class.'

'Mark? The one who sits at the front in Geography?'

'Yeah. He rescued me from some creep who was trying to give me drugs.'

Claire's eyes open wide. 'Drugs? To you?'

'I know.'

Then we both grin and mimic our mothers. 'Just... say... no...' we say together. Then we laugh.

All the hurt from the last week is going.

'I was really lonely,' I say to Claire.

'No you weren't,' she says. 'You had Isabel.'

'She's not like you, though.'

'Did you see her at the party? What did she look like!'

'I know. I thought I was bad at make-up.'

'No, you looked really nice actually,' Claire nods. 'I liked that top you were wearing.'

I gape at her. She can't remember it's the same one I tried on in front of her.

'You said it was a bit revealing last time.'

'Last time?' Claire stares back at me. 'I haven't seen it before.'

'Yes, you have. I tried it on in Dorothy Perkins. You said it wasn't my style.'

'I don't remember saying that. It looks great on you.'

I gape at her. She can't remember it's the same one I tried on in front of her.

I open my mouth to argue, but there's no point. Instead I say, 'Never mind. Shall we go out tomorrow?'

Claire grins. 'Cool idea. Let's go to the cinema.'

'No,' I say. 'I'd like to go shopping.'

'Cassie, we always go shopping. Don't be so boring…'

Here we go again!